Adventures

LEXI

the Giraffe

& Friends.

Lexi Goes
To School

THEODORE H. VALENTINE

AuthorHouse™
1663 Liberty Drive
Bloomington, IN 47403
www.authorhouse.com
Phone: 833-262-8899

ISBN: 978-1-6655-2952-5 (sc)
ISBN: 978-1-6655-2953-2 (e)

Print information available on the last page.

Published by AuthorHouse 06/21/2021

authorHOUSE

Adventures of LEXI the Giraffe & Friends.

Lexi Goes To School

THEODORE H. VALENTINE

Alyssa, the neighbor across the street, sees Lexi with a group of children waiting for the school bus. As the parents talked, the children were laughing and playing with one another.

Bill, the bus driver, pulls up in his big black and yellow school bus. Lexi is the first one on the bus and takes a seat in the back.

Carla, the school bus safety monitor, says, "Calm down children. Bill cannot safely drive the bus until everyone is in their seats and quiet." The bus cautiously pulls away from the curb, as the parents wave goodbye to Lexi and the children.

Down the road came Mrs. Danbury, the school teacher, to meet all the children. Mrs. Danbury was surprised to see Lexi. "I don't remember in all my days of teaching having a giraffe attend our school".

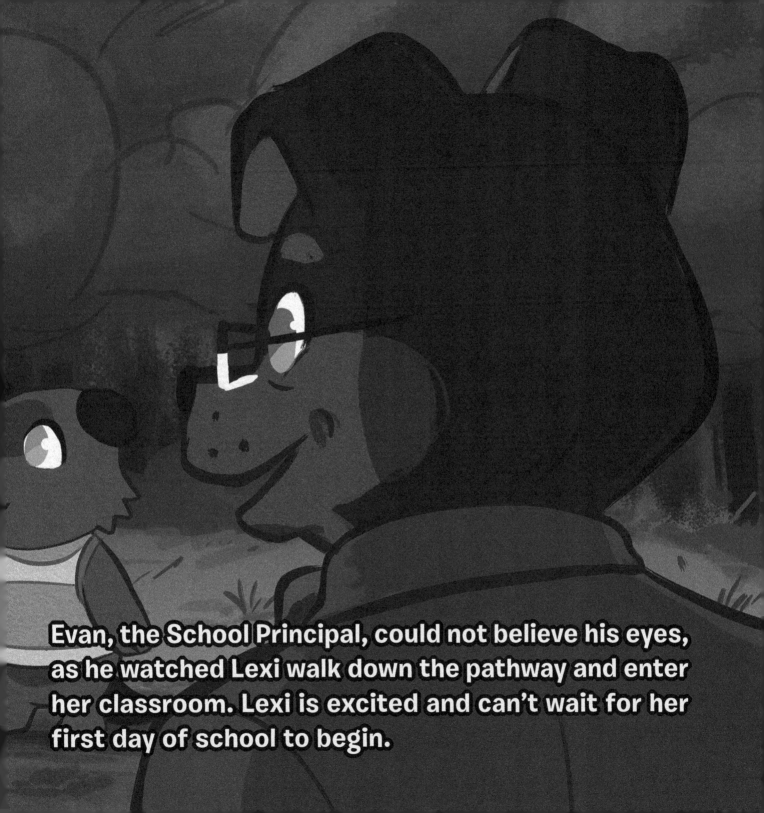

Evan, the School Principal, could not believe his eyes, as he watched Lexi walk down the pathway and enter her classroom. Lexi is excited and can't wait for her first day of school to begin.

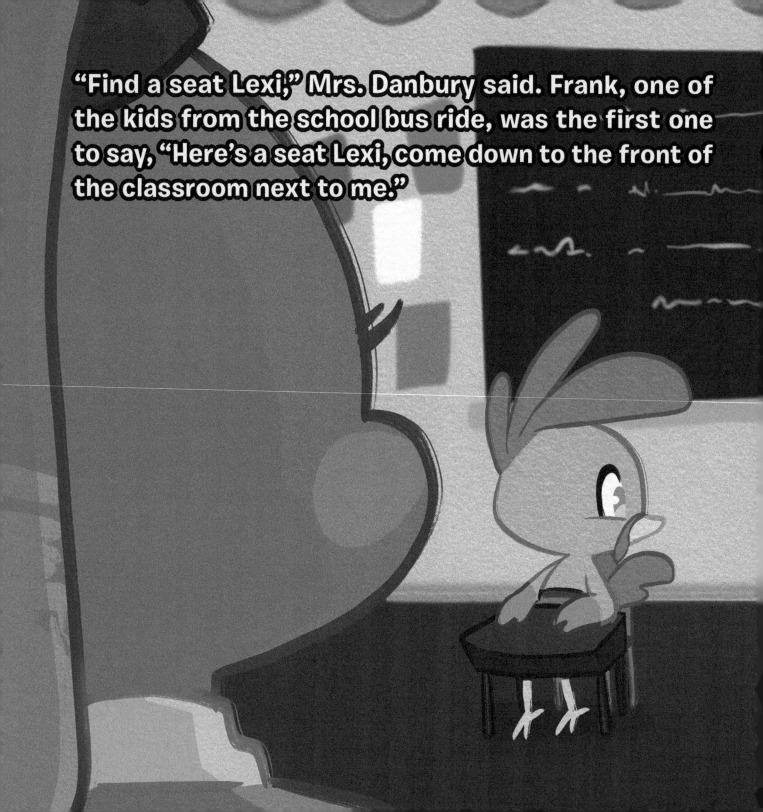

"Find a seat Lexi," Mrs. Danbury said. Frank, one of the kids from the school bus ride, was the first one to say, "Here's a seat Lexi, come down to the front of the classroom next to me."

"Good morning children," said Mrs. Danbury. "Who can tell me a word that starts with the letter G?"

"Lexi!," shouted Gloria, sitting across the classroom. "I mean, Giraffe."

Hira, who was wearing a hat, said, "Lexi doesn't start with the letter G for giraffe". "Correct Hira, you are right," said Mrs. Danbury. Lexi motioned to Hira and then said, "Here is a seat in the front, Hira. Sit here next to me."

"I for Ice," Mrs. Danbury said. "Who would like to say something about Ice? Lexi, how about you?"

"Ice is really cold and it melts very fast if you touch it with your nose," said Lexi.

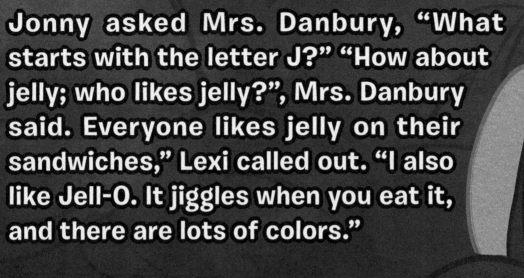

Jonny asked Mrs. Danbury, "What starts with the letter J?" "How about jelly; who likes jelly?", Mrs. Danbury said. Everyone likes jelly on their sandwiches," Lexi called out. "I also like Jell-O. It jiggles when you eat it, and there are lots of colors."

Krystal is one of the kindest kids in school, and everyone says she is the queen of kickball. Krystal asked Lexi to sit with her at lunch. Lexi was excited to tell Krystal all about her experiences.

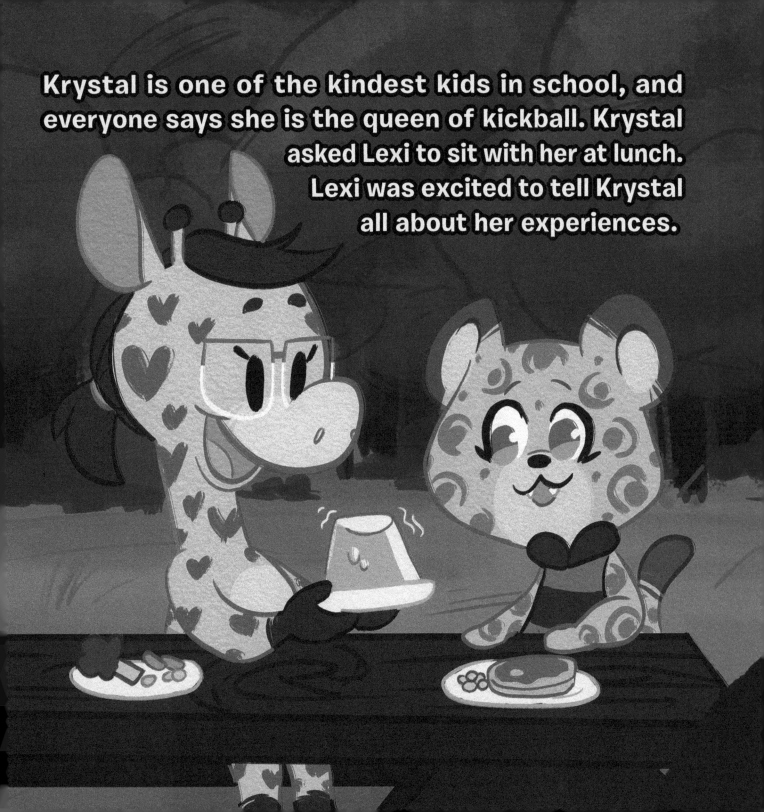

Lunch time did not seem long enough because Lexi was having so much fun telling Krystal all the stories of people and animals she has met and learning more about Krystal's life.

"Math! Mrs. Danbury is starting with math after lunch," said Lexi. "That is one of my favorite subjects. I remember spending most of my days counting the animals when I lived in the jungle."

"No way! No way Mrs. Danbury. There was no way any of the animals could hide from me," said Lexi. "All I had to do was stretch my neck up as high as I could, and I could see everything."

"Oh, what about an Ostrich Lexi; they have a long neck too?" "You're right Omar. An Ostrich does have a long neck, but our neck is the longest of all the other animals; unless you want to count the Brontosaurus," said Lexi.

"Please, everyone turn to page 16 in your books. This would be a great time to talk about the Porcupine," said Mrs. Danbury. "Lexi, could you read the first paragraph?"

"Quickly children, move down the hallway. Quiet children stay in a single file line," said the voice coming out of the hall monitors. There was no question that there was a fire drill. "All children please move out of the building and on to the play yard."

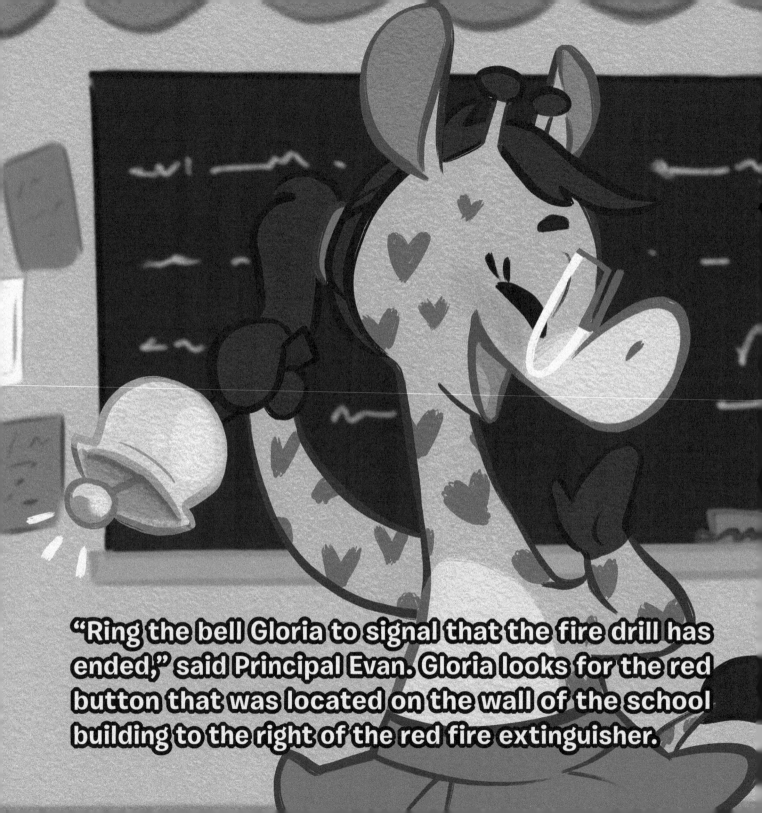

"Ring the bell Gloria to signal that the fire drill has ended," said Principal Evan. Gloria looks for the red button that was located on the wall of the school building to the right of the red fire extinguisher.

"Switch on the lights Gloria. It's time to start our computer science lesson. A very special person donated computers to the school for everyone to use," said Mrs. Danbury.

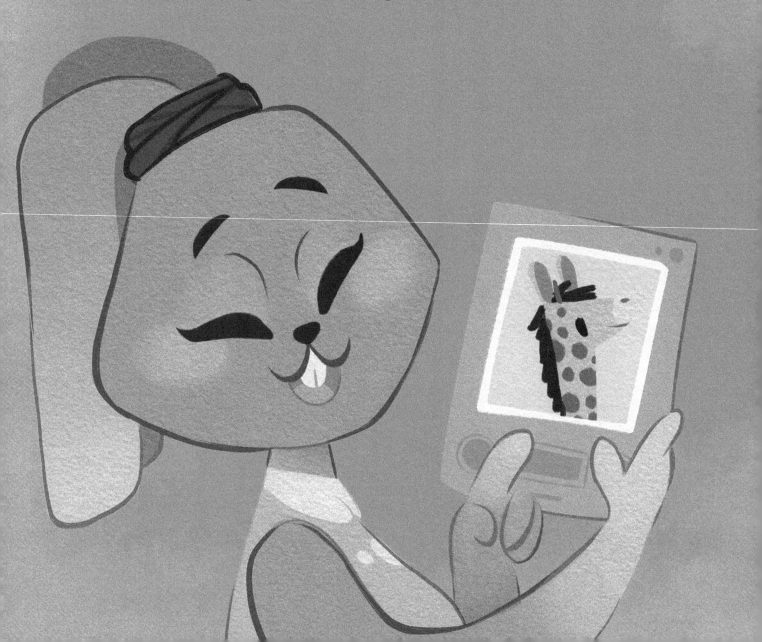

"Thirty computers were delivered today, thanks to Lexi," Mrs. Danbury said. "Lexi, please help all the children set up their computers."

"Under the word "computer" there should be a picture of Lexi in the dictionary. Lexi is unique when it comes to computers, and she says, 'computers unlock the future of the world'", said Mrs. Danbury.

"Virus, void and void!" screamed Lexi. I think the original inventor is looking at us and having a great big laugh," Lexi said.

"Well! This has been a wonderful first day of school. I'm looking forward to seeing everyone again tomorrow," said Mrs. Danbury.

"X marks the spot," Lexi said. "I'm going to use my red chalk and make a big X right where I think bus driver Bill will stop to pick us up."

"You two," said Bill, the school bus driver. "Pick me, pick me," said Lexi and Frank. "Yes, you two will be the assistant school bus monitors on the ride home," said Bill.

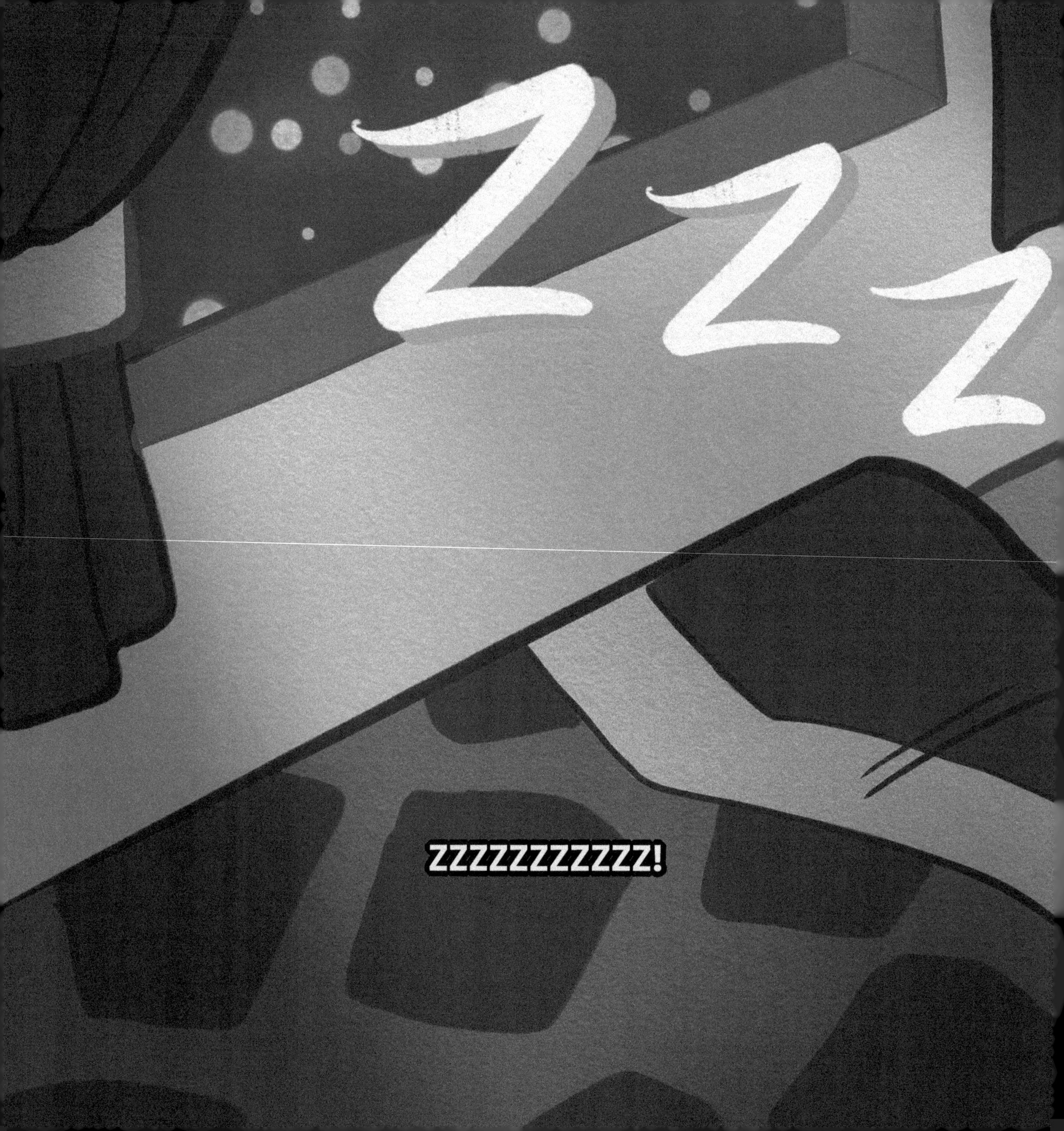
Z Z Z
ZZZZZZZZZZZ!

About the Book

The Adventures of Lexi the Giraffe & Friends, is to be a series of books written to entertain and give children an early introduction to the alphabets, numbers and experiences through the exciting daily lives of Lexi and her friends. Children as well as parents will discover teachable moments, animals, places and ideas that will create hours of enjoyment.

Bio

Author: Theodore H. Valentine,
Published author, entrepreneur, devoted father and husband of 44 years.

Illustrator: Alexia Valentine,
Graduate of Laguna College of Art and Design, with a BFA in animation. Established animator, professional designer and lover of animals big or small.

Editor: Sandra Valentine,
Academic Scholar Pepperdine University, Master's Degree in Business Administration, retired local government analyst, dedicated mother and wife of 44 years.

Project Inspired by: Krystal Valentine,
Inspiration for the book series, successful business woman and loving mother.

CPSIA information can be obtained
at www.ICGtesting.com
Printed in the USA
BVHW021414211221
624588BV00009B/524